NL

♥ Mindy Kim and the ♥
Big Pizza Challenge

**Don't miss more fun adventures
with Mindy Kim!**

Mindy Kim

and the
Big Pizza Challenge

BOOK
6

By Lyla Lee
Illustrated by Dung Ho

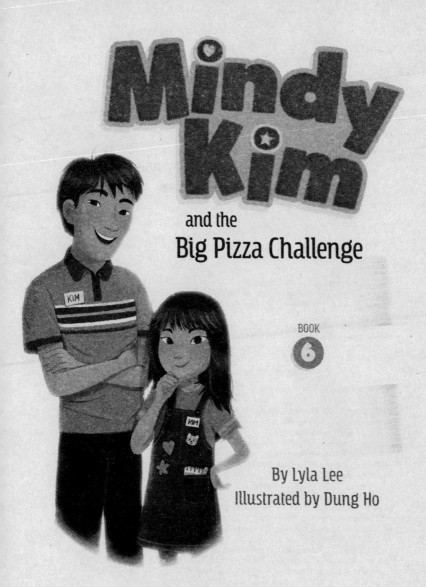

ALADDIN
New York London Toronto Sydney New Delhi

🕊 ALADDIN
An imprint of Simon & Schuster Children's Publishing Division
1230 Avenue of the Americas, New York, New York 10020
First Aladdin paperback edition September 2021
Text copyright © 2021 by Lyla Lee
Illustrations copyright © 2021 by Dung Ho
Also available in an Aladdin hardcover edition.
All rights reserved, including the right of reproduction in whole or in part in any form.
ALADDIN and related logo are registered trademarks of Simon & Schuster, Inc.
For information about special discounts for bulk purchases, please contact Simon & Schuster Special Sales at 1-866-506-1949 or business@simonandschuster.com.
The Simon & Schuster Speakers Bureau can bring authors to your live event. For more information or to book an event contact the Simon & Schuster Speakers Bureau at 1-866-248-3049 or visit our website at www.simonspeakers.com.
Designed by Laura Lyn DiSiena
The illustrations for this book were rendered digitally.
The text of this book was set in Haboro.
Manufactured in the United States of America 0821 OFF
10 9 8 7 6 5 4 3 2 1
Library of Congress Control Number 2021935005
ISBN 978-1-5344-8898-4 (hc)
ISBN 978-1-5344-8897-7 (pbk)
ISBN 978-1-5344-8899-1 (ebook)

For families of all shapes and sizes

Mindy Kim and the
Big Pizza Challenge

Chapter 1

My name is Mindy Kim. I am nine years old, and I'm now in fourth grade!

Ms. Harris, our teacher, is really nice. She tells us fun stories and encourages us to read every day. In fourth grade, we're doing lots of cool projects like learning about the different Native American tribes in Florida and a bunch of other fun stuff too!

One day, Ms. Harris had a big announcement for the entire class.

"In two and a half weeks, our school is going to have a family trivia night for the fourth and fifth graders to help the PTA! The grand prize is a year's worth of pizza from Signor Morelli's Pizza, one of our PTA's sponsors!"

"Free pizza!" exclaimed Brandon, one of the boys in our class. "Free, *unlimited* pizza!"

"I'm going to win the pizza!" yelled another boy.

"No, *I* am!" shouted someone else.

"It's technically only a year's worth," interrupted my friend Sally, pushing up her glasses with one hand. "But that's still a lot of pizza!"

Everyone was really excited. And I was too! I love pizza, and Signor Morelli's has the best pepperoni and stuffed-crust pizzas! My mouth drooled just thinking about them.

Ms. Harris waited for the class to get settled down before continuing. "I sent out an e-mail about buying tickets for the event. You and your parents are all invited to participate!"

All my excitement fizzled out when Ms. Harris said "parents." I just had Dad, and I wasn't sure if he and I could compete with everyone else's parents.

"My family won Trivia Night on both the years when my sisters were at Wishbone," said Sally. "We're really good at trivia!"

She smiled at me, but then she frowned when she saw the look on my face. "Mindy, are you okay?"

I looked down at my feet. "I don't know how much of a chance Dad and I will have. It's just the two of us, and neither of us is good at trivia."

Sally looked sorry for me. But then she perked up. "You and your dad could join our team! If it's anything like the way things were when my sisters went to school here, they group people into teams based on the table they're sitting at, not just by family."

"Really?" I asked. "Your family wouldn't mind?"

"Nope! The more the merrier! And you should also invite Julie!" she exclaimed, waggling her eyebrows. "It'd be an awesome opportunity for some more *family bonding time*."

Julie is my dad's girlfriend. She isn't an official

part of the family yet, but she is really nice, and I like her a lot. From the very beginning, Sally was Dad and Julie's number one fan. She *really* likes romance.

"You guys should still study really hard, though," continued Sally. "And there's a chance they might do things differently this year. I can ask my sisters to tell us what kind of questions they usually ask!"

Sally's enthusiasm was contagious, and soon I was excited all over again.

"That'd be awesome!" I said. "Thanks, Sally!"

"No problem! Just be sure to work as hard as you can. We want to win that pizza for sure!"

Sally and I shook hands. There was no way I was going to let my best friend down!

Chapter 2

That evening, Dad and I were having dinner when I told him about Trivia Night.

"I saw the e-mail!" Dad said. "It looks really fun. Do you want to compete, Mindy?"

"Yeah!" I said. "All that pizza sounds so good!"

"Hmm, I guess it'd make meal planning easier for us if we did win," Dad replied thoughtfully. "I heard we only get one free pizza per month, though. But that's definitely better than nothing!"

I nodded. "It's good that we don't get free pizza every day. If we had pizza every day, we'd get a big stomachache!"

Dad laughed. "That's true! All that oil, grease, and cheese isn't good for you if you eat it too often. Okay, we can try competing if you want to."

"Hooray!"

"But just so you know, since I wasn't born here like you were, there's probably a lot of stuff I won't know about. And work is busy as usual. But I'll still try my best to do whatever I can. Is that okay with you, Mindy?"

"Yeah!" I said. "I can study extra hard for the two of us! And I can ask Eunice for help! Sally said we could join her family's team if we promise to work hard. We can study the things you don't know together, Appa!"

Appa is the Korean word for "Daddy." I was born in San Francisco, but Dad came to the United States when he was in college. His English is good, since he learned it in Korea, but he didn't learn a lot about the American Revolution or other things I'm learning in school, so I have to ask Eunice, my

babysitter, for a lot of homework help instead. And he doesn't exactly keep up with all the new movies and stuff either. Dad and I had a lot of work to do!

Dad smiled. "Okay, Mindy. I'll buy us the tickets. It's so good to see you excited for this! Who knew pizza could be such a big motivator?"

Even though I really liked pizza, I had a secret reason for wanting to win. I wanted to prove that just because I only had one parent, it didn't mean we couldn't do the things that other families could do. We were our own happy family, and we were just as smart, too! And we had friends like Julie and Sally's family to help us.

At that moment, my dog, Theodore the Mutt, barked. I've trained him to not beg at the table anymore, but sometimes he still barks when he wants attention!

I looked down at where Theodore was sitting at my feet.

"Okay, boy, I'll play with you after dinner! But

then I have to go study some trivia! Dad, can I use your tablet? Sally said she'd send me topics I can study for Trivia Night."

"Sure! Just make sure you finish all your home-work first."

"Okay!"

I got up from the table, put my plate in the sink, and threw Theodore's ball. He ran after the ball like one happy camper!

I threw the ball for him a few times before going up to my room to finish my homework. Then I got Dad's tablet and opened up the file that Sally had sent me over e-mail. It was titled TRIVIA NIGHT FUN! and had a *long* list of topics ranging from plate tectonics to the Rock & Roll Hall of Fame! Some things I remembered learn-ing about in school, but others I'd never heard of before.

As I was looking through the list, I heard squeaky noises as Dad played with Theodore. A couple of minutes later, Theodore came upstairs to cuddle with me on my bed, all tired out.

I gave him a pat on the head.

"We have a lot of work to do, Theodore," I told my dog as I looked up the first topic on Dad's tablet. "Here we go!"

Chapter 3

The next day during recess, Sally and I sat at the picnic tables near the playground to work on our homework. I don't usually do homework during school, but I wanted as much time as possible after school to study up for the big competition!

We were both working on our science homework, labeling the parts of the heart. It was pretty easy, so it didn't take long.

"I can ask you a few questions, if you want," said Sally after we finished. "What is the largest mammal in the world?"

"Easy, blue whale!" I said. "I learned about blue

whales in a nature documentary I watched with Dad!"

"Nice! You try asking me a question."

I thought long and hard, trying to come up with something that Sally probably didn't know.

"Who was the first teddy bear named after?"

Sally frowned, deep in thought. "Oh! I know–Theodore 'Teddy' Roosevelt! You named your dog after him, right?"

Darn! She was good.

"Ooh, I have a hard one," Sally said. "Which two countries share the world's longest border? Martha told me they asked this during her trivia night when *she* was in fourth grade."

Martha is Sally's oldest sister. She's in tenth grade, and she's supersmart!

"Um . . ." I thought back to the map of Asia I saw on the plane when I visited Korea with Dad and Julie. "Russia and China!"

Sally made a buzzer sound. "Nope! It's Canada and the US!"

I frowned. I hadn't even thought about this side of the world!

Sally patted my hand when she saw the look on my face. "It's okay," she said. "There's still plenty of time left before Trivia Night! Just study a lot more! Have you thought of asking other people for help? My parents and my sisters are helping me a lot."

I knew Dad, Julie, and Eunice were there for me, but I had mostly been trying to study all by myself until now.

It was time to ask for help!

Chapter 4

On Friday, when Julie came over for dinner, I asked her if she could help Dad and me with Trivia Night practice.

"Sure!" replied Julie. "I love trivia!"

"Let's all practice together after we eat, Mindy," Dad said. "I got us some delicious tteokbokki from the Korean market!"

"Yay, tteokbokki!" I yelled.

Tteokbokki is rice cakes with fish cakes, eggs, and green onions stir-fried in sweet and spicy sauce. It's one of my favorite Korean foods! I like having Julie over for dinner, but the best part is that Dad always buys something yummy whenever she comes over.

We all sat down to eat tteokbokki while asking one another about our week. When it was my turn, I gave Julie the full explanation about Trivia Night and how Sally and I *had to win*.

Julie laughed. "No pressure," she joked. "But okay, let's try our best!"

Dad gave her a grateful look. I was thankful for Julie too! She was so nice.

After we finished eating, we all went to the living room to sit on the couch. Julie got out her phone while Dad got out his tablet. I sat in between them with Theodore. It was super cozy!

"Okay, I'll start us off," Julie said. "What country is also a continent?"

"Australia!" both Dad and I said.

"Yup, great job, you two!" Julie said. "I think that was a pretty easy one, though. Okay, next one. Which famous pop star was nominated for the Best

Actress Oscar in 2019 for her performance in *A Star Is Born*? Ooh, I loved this movie!"

"Britney Spears?" Dad guessed.

"Nope, it's Lady Gaga!" I said. Eunice is a big fan of her music!

"Yup, good job, Mindy!" Julie said, giving me a high five. "She's an amazing actress as well as a singer! Okay, here's an easy one. What country is the Statue of Liberty from?"

"France!" I yelled out, at the same time Dad exclaimed, "Italy!"

"It's France!" Julie said. "It was a gift of friendship from the French."

"Yeah," I replied. "We learned about it in third grade."

"Oof, sorry, Mindy," Dad said, his cheeks turning red. "I don't really know American history very well. I only know Korean history, since that's what I learned in school."

"It's okay, Appa," I said. "I can answer the history

questions for us. And the pop-culture ones! Too bad they probably won't ask any questions about Korean history!"

"Thanks, Mindy. I'll try my best to pull my weight with the science and math questions instead!"

"Okay, then, I have a good science question for you two," Julie said. "What is the hardest substance in the human body?"

I thought for a long time, but I couldn't think of anything. I knew it had to be some kind of bone, but weren't they all equally hard?

Dad jumped up from the couch and answered, "Your teeth! The enamel in them is harder than regular bone."

Julie jumped up too and gave Dad a high five. "Correct! Good job, Brian!"

"Yeah! Good job, Dad!"

I leaped up from the couch and high-fived Julie and Dad too. I was so happy that Dad finally got a correct answer!

"You know, this is actually perfect!" Julie said. "Mindy can answer all the history and English questions, while Brian can answer the science and math ones! And I can help Mindy answer the pop-culture questions and whatever else you two can't get. We're the perfect team!"

We all cheered and got into a group hug. We just might have a chance to win!

Chapter 5

That following Monday after school, Eunice, my babysitter, picked me up as always. My backpack was super heavy, so she had to help me lift it into the car.

"Whoa, what are all these books for, Mindy?" Eunice asked.

"They're for Trivia Night!" I explained. "I can't use Dad's tablet when he's at work, so I borrowed books from the school library. That way I can study when he's not home, too!"

"Oh yeah, your dad told me about that! It's coming up soon, right?"

I nodded, grabbing a book from my bag and clutching it to my chest as I got into my seat. I didn't want to waste any time, so I was going to read it during the car ride to Eunice's house.

"Your dad told me I should make sure you finish all your homework first, though. And then we can study for Trivia Night together. Does that sound like a plan to you?"

"Yeah!" I replied.

When we arrived at her house, Eunice helped me carry my backpack inside. Her dog, Oliver the Maltese, wagged his tail really hard and jumped up and down at the sight of my backpack. I felt bad. He probably thought there were treats for him inside the bag!

"Sorry, boy," I said. "These are just books!"

Eunice laughed. "It's okay, Mindy. My mom and I always give him too many treats anyway."

We went up to Eunice's room to work on our homework. Today I had to do a worksheet on the states of matter. The diagrams about particles got really confusing at times, but luckily, I had Eunice there to help me!

"I'm actually doing physics homework too! Except high school physics is way more complicated than that." She showed me her high school physics textbook. It was huge! And there were lots of drawings with arrows and letters on the pages that made me dizzy.

"Wow, that looks really hard!" I said. I was glad I didn't have to do Eunice's homework too.

By the time we finished our homework, we were hungry, so we went down to the kitchen. Dad was working late today, so I was staying over at Eunice's for dinner. Eunice's mom was making kimchi stew, which smelled so good!

"Dinner will be ready in a bit," Mrs. Park said. "But in the meantime, you can help yourself to some gotgam and sikhye! They're in the fridge."

"Yay!" I said.

One of the things I love most about fall is persimmons. Even though they're available during other seasons, they're the best in the fall! And persimmons are especially good as gotgam, since the dried fruit snacks are sweet and chewy. Along with sikhye, a sugary rice drink, it really is the perfect fall Korean snack!

Back in Eunice's room, Eunice and I happily munched away. Thanks to the snacks, I was more than ready to tackle some books!

After I'd studied a bit, Eunice asked me a bunch of questions using the books. I didn't remember a lot of the answers, but I did my best.

While we were studying, Oliver the Maltese came into the room. So we took a quick break to play with him. Eunice made Oliver do some really cool tricks like "Dance!" and "Play dead!" so we could give him treats. He was so cute!

I really hoped they would ask about dogs on Trivia Night!

Chapter 6

Dad was busy with work for the rest of the week, but we finally got a chance to sit down and practice for Trivia Night together on Thursday night. But something was different about Dad today.

"What is the closest star to Earth?" I asked Dad.

He didn't reply. Instead he was frowning at something on his laptop.

"Dad?" I asked. "Is everything okay?"

"Hmm? Oh, sorry, Mindy. I got a little distracted."

I got up from my seat to see what Dad was looking at. Dad startled and closed his laptop. But he wasn't quick enough, and I could see what was on his screen.

There were a bunch of pretty rings on the page. Were those . . . *engagement rings*?

I gasped. "Dad! Are those *rings*? Are you going to propose to Julie?"

Dad turned red. He looked really embarrassed! "Mindy, I've been meaning to talk to you about this, and sorry, this isn't exactly how I wanted to bring it up. But yes, I've been meaning to for a while. Julie and I have been talking about it more lately."

He then coughed and straightened up in his seat. "How do you feel about me marrying Julie, Mindy? Is that something you're comfortable with?"

I took a few minutes to think about that. Dad had started dating Julie over a year ago, back when I wasn't even eight. She was so nice, and most importantly, she made Dad and me really happy!

When I didn't say anything, Dad continued,

"Just so you know, she'll never replace your mom. No one can. You don't even have to call her Mom, not if you don't want to. I'd really like it if she could join our family. But I'm okay with not going forward with this if you don't want me to. My number one priority is you."

"Aw, thanks, Appa," I said. "I like Julie, and she makes you really happy. I think she'd be a good addition to the family! Theodore thinks so too. Right, Theodore?"

Theodore the Mutt cocked his head at me, looking very confused.

Dad and I laughed, and I gave Theodore a pat on the head.

"Thanks, Mindy," Dad said, giving me a hug. "I'm so happy to hear that you think that."

When we parted, I clung to Dad's arm.

"I know the ring is really important, but can we go back to studying for Trivia Night?" I asked. "It's next Saturday! I'll help you choose a good ring later!"

Dad laughed. "Sorry, Mindy. I guess I was just really nervous about the whole thing. But you're right. Trivia Night first, proposal later. I promise to be one hundred percent focused from now on. Just don't tell Julie what I'm planning, okay?"

"Okay!" I said with a very serious nod.

"It's the sun, by the way," Dad said. "The closest star to Earth?"

"Yeah, you got it!" I cheered. "Good job, Dad."

Dad smiled. Even after Trivia Night was over, it looked like we'd be getting ready for the biggest question and answer of all!

Chapter 7

When I got to class on the last day before Trivia Night, our classroom was set up differently, with the tables divided into four groups with a buzzer in the middle of each one. The group with my desk had a bright yellow buzzer, but there were also purple, red, and green ones elsewhere in the room.

"Hi, class," Ms. Harris said. "Today is going to be a bit different. Instead of having our regular class routine, we're going to start the day with a practice game of trivia! Hopefully, you've been paying attention in class, because a lot of the material we've learned in the past few months is going to be in the questions, along with some new stuff too! The winning group gets this jar of candy."

Ms. Harris held up a jar full of M&M's, Skittles, Sour Patch Kids, and a bunch of other yummy treats!

We all quickly sat in our seats, eager to play.

Ms. Harris pulled up a PowerPoint presentation. It was colorful and *Jeopardy!*-style, with questions divided into five different categories: Science, History, English, Pop Culture, and Miscellaneous. Each category had four different levels, worth one hundred to four hundred points.

When everyone was seated, Ms. Harris turned off the lights and started the presentation. Exciting music played, and everyone cheered. It was trivia time!

"Okay," Ms. Harris said. "Let's get started. Things are going to be a bit different on the actual Trivia Night, but today, I'm going to choose someone to pick a question. Anyone on any team can hit the buzzer to answer! The first team to hit it has the first chance to answer the question and get the points. If the team gets it wrong, though, then it's a free-for-all for the other teams. Who wants to start us off?"

Before anyone else, Priscilla, one of the girls sitting at the group of tables next to ours, raised her hand. She was the class president last year and is supersmart.

"Priscilla," Ms. Harris said. "Thanks for raising your hand so nicely. How about you get us started by picking a category for us?"

Priscilla eyed the different categories and levels.

"Science for four hundred!"

"Excellent choice!" Ms. Harris clicked on the box, and the slide changed to a question that said: *What is the only kind of rock that floats?*

Brandon slammed his hand down on his red buzzer.

"Yes, Brandon?" Ms. Harris asked.

Brandon yelled, "Sandstone!"

Ms. Harris shook her head. "Sorry, but that is incorrect."

Brandon's team groaned, and he leaned back with a huff.

I tried my hardest to think about what the answer was but couldn't think of it. What were the different types of rock again?

Priscilla hit the buzzer.

"Yes, Priscilla?" asked Ms. Harris.

"Pumice!" she said. "It's formed when lava and water mix and has pockets of gas inside it!"

"That's correct! Four hundred to Team Purple!"

Everyone at Priscilla's table cheered and gave her a high five.

"Ugh, they're already ahead by so much!" Sally said. "We have to catch up!"

We went a few more rounds, with Sally and me managing to each score points for our team. Soon we were second, with Priscilla's team first and Brandon's team third. We were only a few hundred points short of being in the lead!

"Okay," Ms. Harris said. "So, the only categories

left are History for three hundred, English for four hundred, Pop Culture for four hundred, and Miscellaneous for three hundred."

I raised my hand.

Ms. Harris nodded at me. "Mindy, you're up. Go ahead and choose a category."

I bit my lip. Miscellaneous could be anything, so it seemed like a big risk. So I said, "History for three hundred!"

"Good choice!"

The slide said: *Which Founding Father set up the National Treasury?*

I gulped. I didn't know the Founding Fathers too well. I wanted to win, though, so I hit the buzzer before anyone else.

"Um," I said. I looked to Sally, who also shrugged. "John Adams?"

Ms. Harris shook her head. "Sorry, Mindy, that is incorrect. Good guess, though!"

Immediately, Brandon slammed his fist on the buzzer.

"ALEXANDER HAMILTON!" he yelled.

"Correct!" said Ms. Harris. "Three hundred points for Team Red."

"Shoot!" I said.

"That was such an easy question!" Brandon yelled at me. "How can you get that wrong? There's an entire musical named after him! My parents and I went to watch it on Broadway!"

I sank down in my seat. Dad was too busy working for us to go to musicals, and definitely to go somewhere as far away as Broadway. And neither of us knew much about American pop culture, either. I only listened to the Korean pop music that I got from Eunice!

"That's quite enough, Brandon," said Ms. Harris.

Sally patted me on the back. "It's okay, Mindy," she said. "We can catch up!"

But as the game went on, our team only fell further and further behind. By the end, I felt so bad. We'd been doing so well until I got that question wrong!

Priscilla's team was in the lead for the most part, but at the very last question, Brandon's team won with a stroke of luck!

When his team went up to the front of the class to get the jar of treats, Brandon stuck his tongue out at me.

"Why bother even showing up at Trivia Night? I'm still going to beat you!"

"Don't listen to him, Mindy!" said Sally. "With the combined brainpower of your family and mine, we'll *definitely* beat his team."

Sally's words made me feel a bit better, but I still clenched my fists. Brandon was so mean, and he made me so mad! I was more determined than ever to win Trivia Night.

Chapter 8

That night, instead of reading our usual bedtime story, Dad and I quizzed each other on trivia questions that he found on his tablet. There were a lot more questions I didn't know than I'd hoped, and I felt super discouraged, especially after what had happened in class.

I thought about just giving up. I felt so bad for wasting Dad's time!

Dad must have noticed my bad mood, because he frowned and patted my head.

"You okay, kiddo?" he asked. "You don't seem to be having as much fun with these as you usually do."

I sighed. "I don't think we're going to win tomorrow. We practiced in class today and Brandon's team beat us by a lot! Sally's family is good, and we're working really hard too, but what if we still can't win against the other teams? I got a really easy question wrong during class, too, one that almost everyone knew. Sorry for wasting your time, Appa."

Dad put aside his tablet so he could pull me into a hug.

"Aw, Mindy. I'm sorry that happened," he said. "But please know that you didn't waste my time at all! Don't ever think that. First of all, no matter how hard we try, it's nearly impossible for anyone to know the answers to all the trivia questions! So I don't want you to feel bad about that. Second, I've really enjoyed preparing for this with you. And I hope you've had a good time too! Yeah, the pizza prize is great, but the most important part of all this is how much you're learning and that you're

having fun, right? What's the point of trying to win pizza if you're miserable?"

Dad had a good point.

"True," I said. "Even pizza doesn't taste as good when you're sad."

Dad laughed. "That reminds me. Did I tell you about that one time you were four and Mom gave you pizza? You were mad because we cut your playtime short so we could sit down for dinner. And you ended up throwing the slice at your mom!"

"Oh no!" I said, covering my face with my hands. I was really embarrassed at how mean I was to Mom when I was a little kid. "Really?"

Dad nodded, still smiling. "It's okay, though. Your mom and I thought it was really funny. It left a pizza-shaped stain on Mom's shirt!"

He laughed, so I giggled too. I love it whenever Dad tells me a new story about Mom.

"So, honestly, don't worry about us winning. I can always get you pizza, Mindy. Even if it's not as much as the prize amount. It's not the pizza that's important—it's the time we spend preparing together, okay? And I'd rather you have a good time than worry about winning. Why do you want to win so much, anyway? We get pizza all the time."

I sighed. I wasn't sure if I should tell Dad my *real* reasons for wanting to win Trivia Night because I didn't want to hurt his feelings.

Dad frowned. "What is it?"

I looked down and said, "I wanted to prove that our family is just as good as everyone else's."

"Oh, Mindy." Dad squeezed me tight again. "You know our family is good enough on its own, right? Or do you feel like it's not enough?"

I shook my head. "No, I like our family! You, me, Theodore the Mutt, and now Julie! But it's different from the other kids who have both parents. Like Sally!"

Dad sighed. "I understand. But different isn't bad, right? Besides, wouldn't it be weird if everyone came from the same families? We'd all be clones! Or robots!" He crossed his eyes and went, "Bee-boop, bee-boop," like a machine!

I giggled. Dad is so silly.

"We'll do amazing," he said, giving me a kiss on my forehead. "Whether we win or not, we both worked so hard on this. *You* worked *really* hard on this, Mindy, even studying things that are *way* beyond your grade level! I am so proud and impressed—you have no idea. You're so smart! Mom would be very proud of you too."

I smiled. I was crying, not because I was sad, but because I was happy, and I missed Mom. "Thanks, Appa. Good night."

"Good night."

Dad turned off the light and I went to sleep, tucked in between Theodore the Mutt and my stuffed animals.

Chapter 9

In my dreams that night, Dad and I went to Signor Morelli's Pizza. But when we got there, Mom and Julie were there too, waiting for us with a large and yummy pepperoni pizza!

"Mindy!" Mom said, a bright smile on her face. "Where have you guys been? We've been waiting a long time."

"Woof! Woof!" I looked down to see that Theodore the Mutt was there too, wagging his tail beneath the table. The whole family was here!

I looked from Julie to Mom, and they smiled at each other. Julie and Mom were talking and

laughing like they were friends. It made me really happy to see them together like that.

"Let's sit down, Mindy," Dad said, pulling out a chair for me. "I bet you're hungry after the long day at school!"

The four of us talked as we ate the pizza. Everyone was laughing and I was so happy, my heart felt like it was going to burst. Theodore the Mutt participated in the conversation too, begging for scraps and making everyone smile with his cuteness.

When we were done eating, Mom gave me a big, tight hug, like she always did when I was little.

I was crying when I woke up, but I was smiling, too. I felt really hopeful! I hoped the dream meant that Mom was watching over us, happy and proud of Dad and me for working so hard for Trivia Night.

I jumped out of bed, and the real Theodore the Mutt barked in excitement.

"Come on, Theodore!" I said. "It's Trivia Day!"

I ran downstairs with Theodore close behind. Julie and Dad were downstairs, making pancakes. Julie must have come over early to help Dad!

I gave both of them a big hug.

"Whoa there," Dad said with a chuckle. "Good morning, kiddo. Sleep well?"

I nodded. "Yeah! I had a really good dream. And I'm so excited about Trivia Night!"

Dad smiled. "Glad to hear it. Win or lose, let's give it our best shot, okay?"

"Okay!"

"You guys will do great," Julie said. "I'm sure of it! And I'll be there to help too, of course."

I smiled. Whatever happened tonight, I felt so lucky to have Julie and Dad!

Chapter 10

When it was finally time to head to the school for Trivia Night, I hugged Theodore in my arms real tight before we left.

"Wish us luck, buddy!" I said. "And take good care of the house while we're gone."

Theodore licked my face and wagged his tail.

"Aw, thanks. I love you too!" I giggled and kissed his forehead before putting him back down.

Dad drove us to the school. On the way, everyone was so nervous that no one said anything! It was finally the moment of truth!

When we arrived, the parking lot was full of

cars. Tons of kids were getting out of their cars and walking to the school building with their moms and dads. I wasn't jealous or sad, though. Dad, Theodore, and I were a happy enough family on our own, *and* we had Julie, so our family was *extra* happy!

We walked into the cafeteria, and my jaw almost dropped to the floor! It looked completely different, like it was a whole new place! The tables were covered in pretty tablecloths that were white and sky blue—our school colors. A disco ball lit up the darkness in the middle of the room with rainbow lights. And the projector screen was pulled open onstage, with a PowerPoint slide that said: *Welcome to Wishbone Elementary's eighth annual PTA Trivia Night!*

"Wow!" I exclaimed. "I wish the cafeteria always looked this cool!"

Dad and Julie seemed pretty impressed too. We all glanced around, trying to figure out where we could sit.

"Mindy, over here!"

Sally waved her hands at us from one of the tables, where she was sitting with her sisters and parents. I breathed a sigh of relief. Everyone on our team was here and accounted for!

"Welcome, fourth and fifth graders of Wishbone Elementary, to Trivia Night!" said Dr. Mortimer, our principal, as we made our way to Sally's table. "Thank you to everyone who bought tickets for the event and could make it out tonight. Your contribution helps us make the school great. Please have a seat anywhere at the tables. We will begin shortly."

When we sat down at the table, Sally's sisters and parents said hi to us. Sally has two sisters—Martha and Patricia—who both look like older versions of Sally in different ways. Sally and Patricia both have the same color hair, but Martha's face is more similar to Sally's! Whenever I see Sally's sisters, I wonder what my own siblings would look like if I had any.

Dad and Julie were sitting across from Sally's parents, while I sat across from Sally and her sisters. There was a big sign with a flamingo in front of our table.

"They always name the teams by a random animal," Sally explained. "So we're Team Flamingo!"

I looked around at the other tables. There were many different kinds of animals, including a gorilla, a cheetah, and a polar bear! It was like we were at a zoo!

Ms. Polinsky, the head of the PTA, went up onto the stage.

She explained to everyone how Trivia Night was going to work. It was pretty much the same as how we'd done it in class. The only difference was that there were two rounds, not one!

"About halfway into the night, the members of the PTA and I are going to tally up the points of each team to determine the top four teams," Ms. Polinsky explained. "Then we'll have a lightning round to determine the grand-prize winner! In case you haven't heard, the grand prize this year is a gift certificate for twelve free pizzas–one for each month–at Signor Morelli's, one of our sponsors!"

At the mention of free pizza, all the kids cheered. Even some of the parents did too!

Then Trivia Night began!

"What was the name of the still currently active volcano in Washington State that erupted in 1980?" Ms. Polinsky asked.

Sally slammed her hand on the buzzer.

"Mount Saint Helens!" she said.

"Correct!"

"Yay!" I said. "Good job!"

We were already off to a great start!

The next couple of questions were a lot trickier. And even when our team *did* know the answer, we didn't buzz in fast enough to answer the question!

"No!" said Sally. "We have to be faster!"

"The competition is definitely a lot fiercer this year than the last time we participated!" Mrs. Johnson, Sally's mom, said. "How about we have one designated person to just buzz in automatically each time? That way we'll always have a chance to at least try answering the question!"

"That's a great idea, Mom," said Sally. "I can be that person for our team!"

Next, Ms. Polinsky asked, "What year did Pluto stop being a planet?"

Sally rang the buzzer.

I didn't know the answer! But, luckily, Dad did. He answered, "2006!"

"Correct!"

"Wow, good job, Brian!" said Julie. Everyone at the table praised Dad too. He looked so happy!

"Yay, Dad!" I cheered. I was so proud of him!

We continued like this for another hour, with Sally's parents and sisters getting a good chunk of the questions as well. Then Ms. Polinsky said, "All right, it's time to total up the points so we can narrow down the teams to the top four. Please wait just a moment."

We all waited in hushed anticipation as the PTA members counted up the points.

By the time Ms. Polinsky went back up onto the stage, I was hugging Sally really tight!

"Thank you for your patience!" Ms. Polinsky said with a big smile. "The teams that will move on to the finals are Cheetah, Dragon, Polar Bear, and Flamingo!"

"Yes!" Sally and I cheered.

We looked over at the other teams that had made it past this round.

"Oh no!" I said when I saw one of the teams.

Brandon and his friend Mikey were on Team Polar Bear with their families. Mikey was a big bully in *his* class, so mean that I heard about him at recess.

The other two teams were from other classes, so I didn't know them very well.

"We have to beat Brandon no matter what," I told Sally.

"Agreed!" she said.

Brandon cupped his hands around his mouth and yelled at us from across the cafeteria. "We're going to cream you guys!"

"Oh no you won't!" I yelled back.

"Wow, that kid is really mean," said Dad.

"That's Brandon, our class bully," I explained.

Ms. Polinsky opened up a new presentation for the next set of questions.

I bit my lip.

This was it! The final round!

Chapter 11

The first question of the final round was impossibly hard!

"The world's largest coral reef system is the Great Barrier Reef, which is off the coast of Australia," said Ms. Polinsky. "About how many square miles is it in total?"

Sally hit the buzzer.

"Yes, Team Flamingo?"

Sally looked at me. I looked at Dad. And Dad looked at Julie. Julie looked at Mrs. Johnson. Mrs. Johnson looked at Sally's sisters and Mr. Johnson. No one knew the answer!

"Um . . . ," I said.

A girl from Team Cheetah hit the buzzer.

"About a hundred thirty-five thousand square miles!" she said.

"Correct!"

Everyone in the cafeteria clapped.

"How did she know that?" Sally gasped.

I shrugged. I'd studied really hard, but not *that* hard.

"Next question," said Ms. Polinsky. "What is the oldest university in the United States?"

"I KNOW THIS ONE!" Sally buzzed in and bolted up from her seat. "Harvard University! My mom went there!"

Everyone laughed, and Sally's mom blushed.

"Correct!" said Ms. Polinsky.

We were down to the last five questions. Team Polar Bear got the next one, and Brandon stuck his tongue out at us.

"Four questions left!" Ms. Polinsky said. "One more if we need a tiebreaker."

Team Cheetah got another question right after that, and then Ms. Polinsky asked, "What boy band broke multiple Guinness World Records, two of which are for the most viewed YouTube music video in twenty-four hours?"

Sally hit the buzzer, and Julie and I both answered, "BTS!"

"Correct!" Ms. Polinsky said.

We all cheered. Julie and I smiled at each other. After Eunice introduced me to them one day while I was over at her house, I'd told Julie about BTS, and we'd watched a lot of their music videos together since!

We couldn't celebrate for long, though, because then Team Polar Bear scored the next points. We were tied, and there was only one question left!

"Get ready to lose, suckers!" Brandon yelled.

"That kid is a little rude," Mr. Johnson said. "And the parents, unfortunately, aren't doing anything about it either."

Mr. Johnson was right. Brandon's parents were both on their phones instead of paying attention to what Brandon was doing. I kind of felt bad for Brandon. I felt really lucky that Dad and Julie were actually participating!

"We can't let them win!" I cried out. "We worked so hard for this!"

"The final question for Trivia Night is . . ." Ms. Polinsky paused dramatically before continuing. "Who was the youngest recipient of the Nobel Peace Prize, and how old was she when she got the award?"

Sally hit the buzzer. For a split second, my mind went completely blank. Everyone else looked stumped too. *Oh no!*

I was about to give up when I remembered a book that Dad and Julie had bought for me during summer vacation.

"Malala Yousafzai," I said. "She was seventeen!"

"Correct!"

Everyone on our team yelled out with joy, and the rest of the cafeteria clapped for us.

Dad lifted me onto his shoulders, beaming with happiness and pride. "Wow, you did it, Mindy! We won Trivia Night!"

"I couldn't have done it without you and Julie!" I said with a big smile. "I remembered learning about Malala in the book you got me!"

"I'm so glad we could help," Julie replied. "Congratulations!"

"Everyone on our team helped!" I said. "I'm so proud of us!"

Confetti rained down from the ceiling and we all hugged one another. Julie and Dad shared a kiss.

Sally waggled her eyebrows at me, and I smiled.

We'd done it! We'd won Trivia Night, and it had been a real family team effort.

And now it was time for pizza!

* * *

Sally's family and mine went to Signor Morelli's right after Trivia Night. It was almost my bedtime, so the restaurant was pretty empty when we got there.

"You guys came in just in time!" the waiter said when we sat down. "Our kitchen is closing soon."

With our prize from Trivia Night, we got one big free pizza for us kids, while Dad and Mr. Johnson split the cost of another one for the adults.

The pizza was so good, and the cheese melted right in my mouth! It was the best pizza I'd ever had, probably because we'd worked so hard to win the prize. Everyone was really happy, and it was the perfect end to a fun night.

On our way out, Dad and Mr. Johnson agreed that our families should evenly split the rest of the prize, so we could have pizza for one month while the Johnsons had it for the other.

"And maybe our families could come together once in a while to do joint pizza nights again!" Dad said.

I smiled. I was happy enough that we won, but the pizza sure was a nice bonus!

Now that Trivia Night was over, it was time to think about the next thing on our plate.

"So . . . Appa, when are you going to propose to Julie?" I asked when Dad tucked me into bed that night.

Dad smiled. "Well, I have a plan for what I want to do, but I wanted to wait until after we were done with Trivia Night. . . . I think I'm also a little too chicken to go through with my plan right away."

"Aw, don't be afraid. I'll help!" I said. "You can even cry on my shoulder if she says no."

"Mindy!" Dad laughed. "Do you want her to say no?"

"I was just kidding. But seriously, Dad, what are you waiting for? Now that Trivia Night is over, you have no excuse."

Dad gave me a nervous smile. "You're right, Mindy. Okay, let's plan for next weekend if the weather is nice. Maybe we can take her to the neighborhood park since it's beautiful over there. Do you and Theodore want to help?"

"You bet!" I said. "And I'm sure Sally would love to help out too!"

Dad laughed and ruffled my hair. "Thanks, kiddo. I am lucky to have you. You know that, right? Not only are you hardworking and smart, but you are also really nice. I don't say this enough, but I am proud of you for having adjusted well to our life here in Florida in the past year or so. You always try to be nice to everyone, and I'm constantly so impressed by that."

I grinned. "Thanks, Appa. It's because you're such a good dad!"

Dad hugged me tight. "Aw, thanks for saying that, Mindy. I do try my best, but I can't take full credit. You're an awesome person all on your own!"

I felt really proud of myself then, and happy and thankful for the great day we'd had today.

That night, I went to sleep with a big smile on my face.

Chapter 12

On the day Dad planned to propose to Julie, Dad and I went to the Korean supermarket.

"I want to make sure I get the snacks she likes," Dad said as we walked around the store. "Can you please help me, Mindy?"

He looked super nervous. Dad hadn't even proposed yet, and he was already sweating!

"Julie loves Pepero and Choco Pies!" I said. "She also really likes the shrimp crackers."

Dad laughed. "Great! We can get those. Thanks, Mindy!"

Back in the car, Dad put the snacks in the picnic

JULIE
We have a bonus question for you!
WILL YOU BE A PART OF OUR FAMILY?

basket he had stored in the trunk. Our car was full of stuff for the proposal, like balloons and strings of fairy lights! There was also a poster that I'd made with Eunice's help. I wanted to help Dad pop the question!

Next we picked up Theodore the Mutt from the house and went to the park. With all the decorations and both Theodore and me in the back seat, the car ride was a little crowded but still fun!

In the middle of the park there was a pretty gazebo that overlooked a lake, which sparkled under the sunlight. It was so pretty!

The Johnsons met us at the park. Sally, her sisters, and her parents all helped us decorate the gazebo with the balloons and lights. I set out a picnic blanket on the floor, and Dad brought the basket of snacks from the car and placed it in the middle of the blanket.

Then, as a finishing touch, we scattered the gazebo floor with a bunch of pink flower petals. Theodore tried eating a couple, but I shooed him away.

"No, bad dog!" I yelled. "Dogs aren't supposed to eat flowers!"

Theodore's ears drooped. He looked really sad and sorry. I felt bad for yelling at him, so I gave him a bone so he could chew on it instead.

By the time we were done preparing, the sun was about to set. I set candles in a heart shape and Dad lit them one by one.

Finally, it was time for Dad to go get Julie.

Dad was so nervous that his hands were shaking. He was really pale, too! He took a long, deep breath before getting back into his car.

"It's okay, Appa," I said. "You can do it! She's going to say yes for sure!"

"Thanks, Mindy," Dad replied. "I'm so nervous!"

I was nervous too. I liked Julie, but Dad getting married to Julie meant that our lives were going to change. And change is kind of scary, even when it's good!

But all my nervousness blew away when Dad came back with Julie. Sally and her family took out their phones so they could take pictures and videos of the proposal, while I held out the poster I'd made with Eunice. It had a picture I drew of Julie, Theodore, Dad, and me on it, and said, *Julie, we have a bonus question for you! Will you be a part of our family?*

The moment Julie saw my poster and the gazebo, her eyes started tearing up.

She cried even more happy tears when Dad got on one knee and showed her the ring.

"Julie," Dad said. "You've been such a bright spot in both Mindy's life and mine, and I am honored to know you. Words can't express how much I love and appreciate you. I would be so happy if you could be my wife. . . ." Dad paused to smile at me and my poster. "Mindy, Theodore, and I would love you to *officially* join our family. Will you marry me?"

"Brian, of course I'd love to be your wife," replied Julie, laughing and crying at the same time. She turned to look at me, wiping tears away from her eyes. "And your stepmom, Mindy, if you'll have me."

She reached down to pet Theodore in between his ears. "And yours too, Theodore!"

Theodore closed his eyes and let out a happy sigh. We all laughed.

"We are so lucky to have you!" I said, giving Julie a big hug.

She squeezed me tight and kissed me on the forehead.

"And I'm lucky to have *you*! You two have been

73

such bright spots in my life as well," Julie said. "Before, I was so lonely living here away from my family. Being a part of yours has been one of the highlights of the last year and a half."

Dad smiled. "Well, I'm so glad that you feel the same way."

He was crying happy tears too.

I beamed. "By the way, I hope you like the snacks in the basket. Dad asked me for help on which snacks to buy."

"Of course I will, Mindy!" Julie said with a wink. "You know that good food is the key to my heart. We have that in common!"

Everyone laughed. We were all so happy!

Dad put the ring on Julie's finger and then pulled her in for a kiss.

We cheered and celebrated by eating the yummy snacks.

Dad was getting married, and I couldn't wait for the wedding!

Acknowledgments

My first round of thanks goes to my parents, who always tried their best to help me with my homework and other school activities while I was growing up here in the States. Mindy's story is obviously fictional, but it was inspired in part by how my parents worked hard to support me even when they came from an immigrant background, weren't fluent in English, and weren't familiar with a lot of the concepts I learned in school. Although I ended up Googling most things myself anyway, it's definitely the thought and effort that count! A special shout-out goes to my dad, who spent long hours trying to translate my American textbooks into Korean so he could understand the math and science concepts well enough to explain them to me.

I'd also like to take the time to thank all other immigrant parents out there like Mindy's dad and my parents. Not only do you have to wrestle with the normal challenges of being a parent, but you also have to fight other added challenges such as language barriers, culture clashes, and racism. You work so hard so we can have better lives. I see you and I appreciate you.

Thank you to the usual suspects, aka my friends. I've thanked y'all plenty in the previous Mindy Kim books (like in the one that came out in June, LOL!), so you know who you are. :) Thank you for being my support system throughout the years and for reminding me that there is more to life than just work.

As always, thank you to Penny Moore, my agent,

as well as my amazing team at Simon & Schuster for all that you do to bring Mindy's stories to life. And thank you to the readers, parents, booksellers, librarians, and educators for following Mindy in her adventures and sharing her stories. Mindy and I are so lucky to have friends like you!

Finally, I'd like to thank Sean Dilliard for being such a perfect partner. Thank you for all the hugs, late-night discussions, and endless words of support. Though 2020 was a historically bad year, I'm so grateful that it brought us together.

COMING SOON!

By Lyla Lee

Mindy Kim

and the Fairy-Tale Wedding

illustrated by
Dung Ho

About the Author

Lyla Lee is the author of the Mindy Kim series as well as the YA novel *I'll Be the One*. Although she was born in a small town in South Korea, she's since then lived in various parts of the United States, including California, Florida, and Texas. Inspired by her English teacher, she started writing her own stories in fourth grade and finished her first novel at the age of fourteen. After working various jobs in Hollywood and studying psychology and cinematic arts at the University of Southern California, she now lives in Dallas, Texas. When she is not writing, she is teaching kids, petting cute dogs, and searching for the perfect bowl of shaved ice. You can visit her online at lylaleebooks.com.

Looking for another great book?
Find it
IN THE MIDDLE.

Fun, fantastic books for kids
in the in-be**TWEEN** age.

IntheMiddleBooks.com

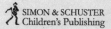